P9-CDO-982

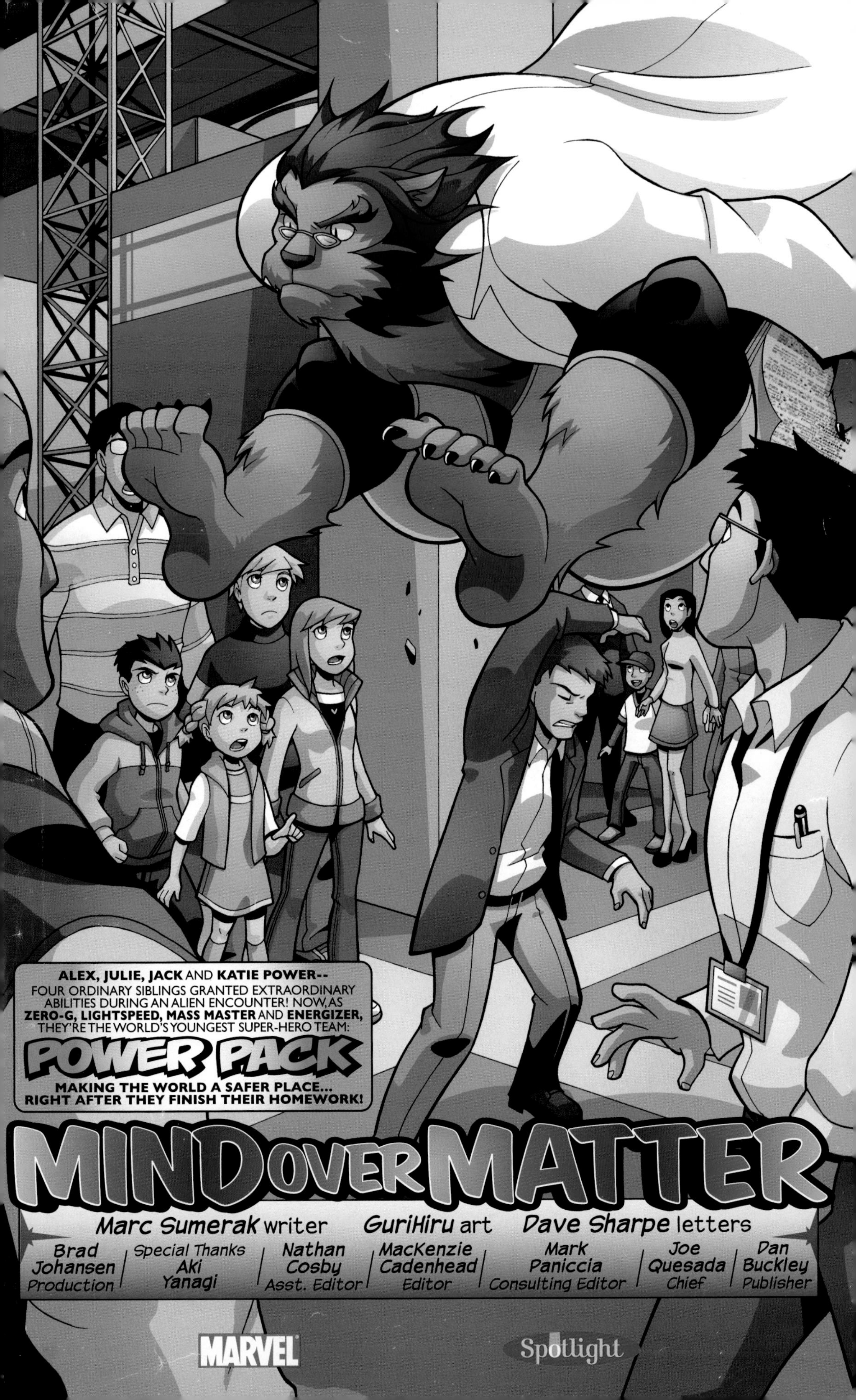
ALEX, JULIE, JACK AND KATIE POWER--
FOUR ORDINARY SIBLINGS GRANTED EXTRAORDINARY ABILITIES DURING AN ALIEN ENCOUNTER! NOW, AS ZERO-G, LIGHTSPEED, MASS MASTER AND ENERGIZER, THEY'RE THE WORLD'S YOUNGEST SUPER-HERO TEAM:
POWER PACK
MAKING THE WORLD A SAFER PLACE... RIGHT AFTER THEY FINISH THEIR HOMEWORK!
MIND OVER MATTER
Marc Sumerak writer
GuriHiru art
Dave Sharpe letters
Brad Johansen Production
Special Thanks Aki Yanagi
Nathan Cosby Asst. Editor
MacKenzie Cadenhead Editor
Mark Paniccia Consulting Editor
Joe Quesada Chief
Dan Buckley Publisher
MARVEL
Spotlight

VISIT US AT
www.abdopublishing.com

Spotlight library bound edition © 2007. Spotlight is a division of ABDO Publishing Company, Edina, Minnesota.

Cataloging Data

Sumerak, Marc
   Mind over matter / Marc Sumerak, writer ; GuriHiru, art ; Dave Sharpe, letters. -- Library bound ed.
      p. cm. -- (X-Men power pack)
   Summary: Marvel's youngest superheroes Alex, Julie, Jack, and Katie team up with their idols Wolverine, Cyclops, and other X-Men to keep the world a safer place.
   "Marvel age"--Cover.
   Revision of the January 2006 issue of Marvel age X-Men Power Pack.
   ISBN-13: 978-1-59961-222-5
   ISBN-10: 1-59961-222-4
   1. Superheroes (Fictitious characters)--Comic books, strips, etc.--Fiction.
   2. Graphic novels. I. Title. II. Series.

741.5dc22

All Spotlight books are reinforced library binding and manufactured in the United States of America

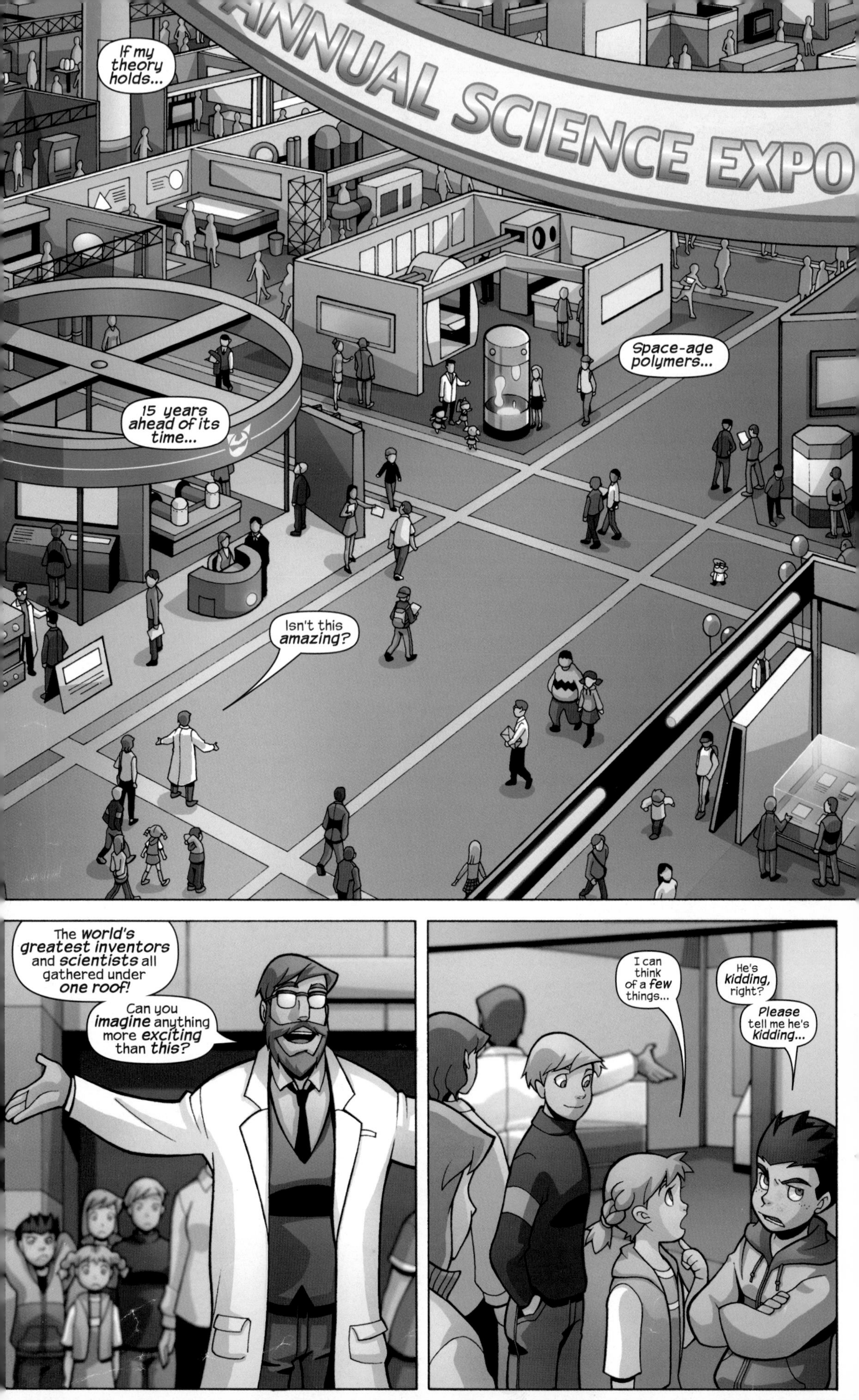
ANNUAL SCIENCE EXPO
If my theory holds...
15 years ahead of its time...
Space-age polymers...
Isn't this amazing?
The world's greatest inventors and scientists all gathered under one roof!
Can you imagine anything more exciting than this?
I can think of a few things...
He's kidding, right?
Please tell me he's kidding...

I'm going to get your *father* to his *booth* before he *bursts* with *excitement*.

Ooh! That *reminds* me! There's a seminar on *spontaneous combustion* at 3:30...

You kids can go *look around*... just *try* not to *have too much fun*, okay?

I *don't think* you need to worry about *that*, Mom!

Ugh. Can you *believe* that we're stuck at this *nerd-fest* all day?

Who are you trying to *kid*, Julie?

Your *clothes* may have gotten *trendier*, but you're still the *family bookworm!*

Just because I'm *acing chemistry class* doesn't mean I *enjoy* it, Jack.

I mean, when am I *ever* gonna need to use *any* of *this stuff* in--

--in our "line of work"?

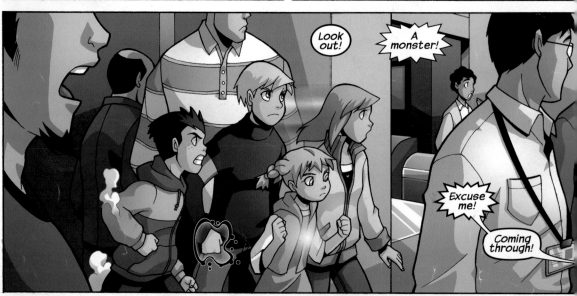

Look out!

A *monster!*

Excuse me!

Coming through!

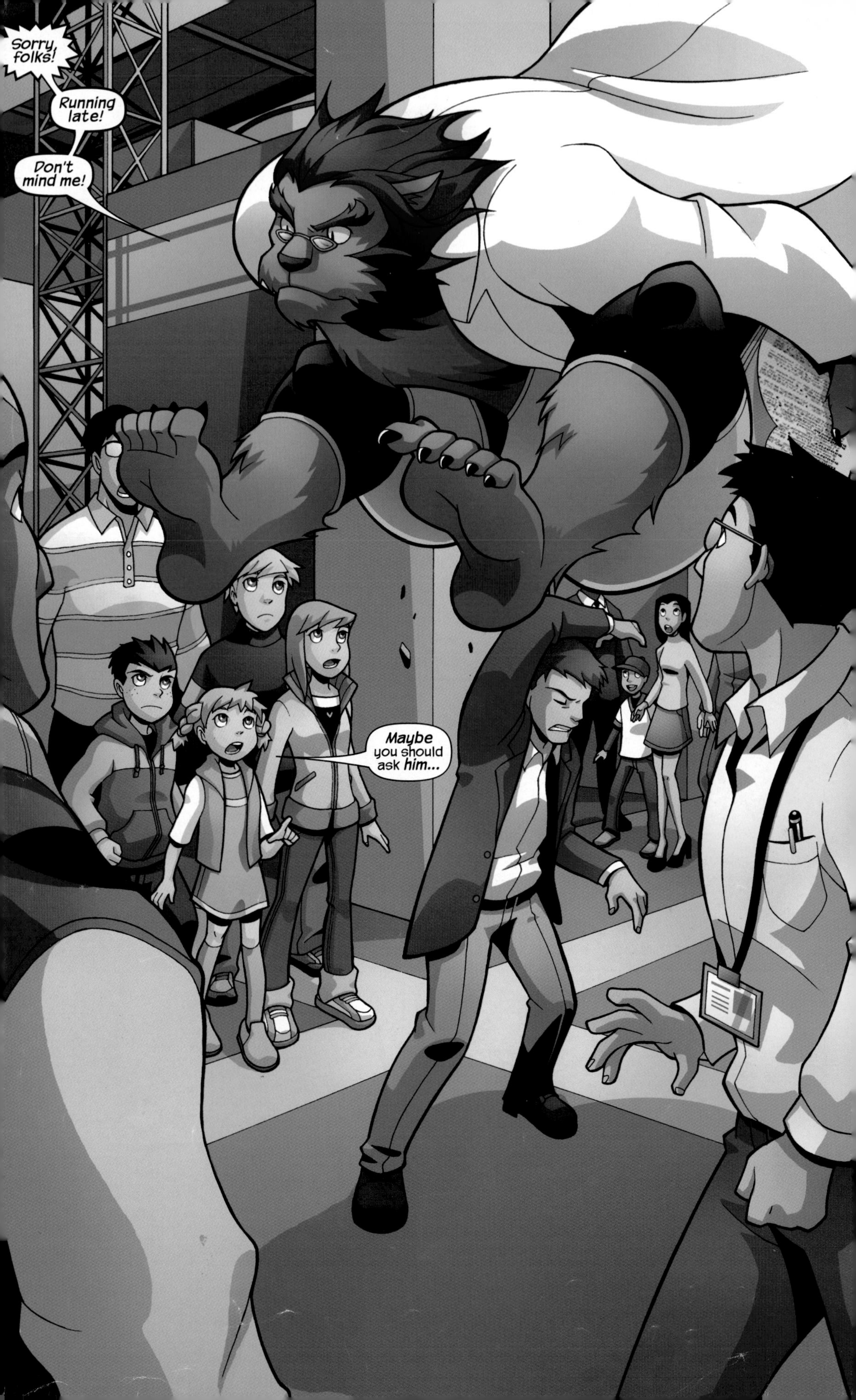
Sorry, folks!
Running late!
Don't mind me!
Maybe you should ask him...

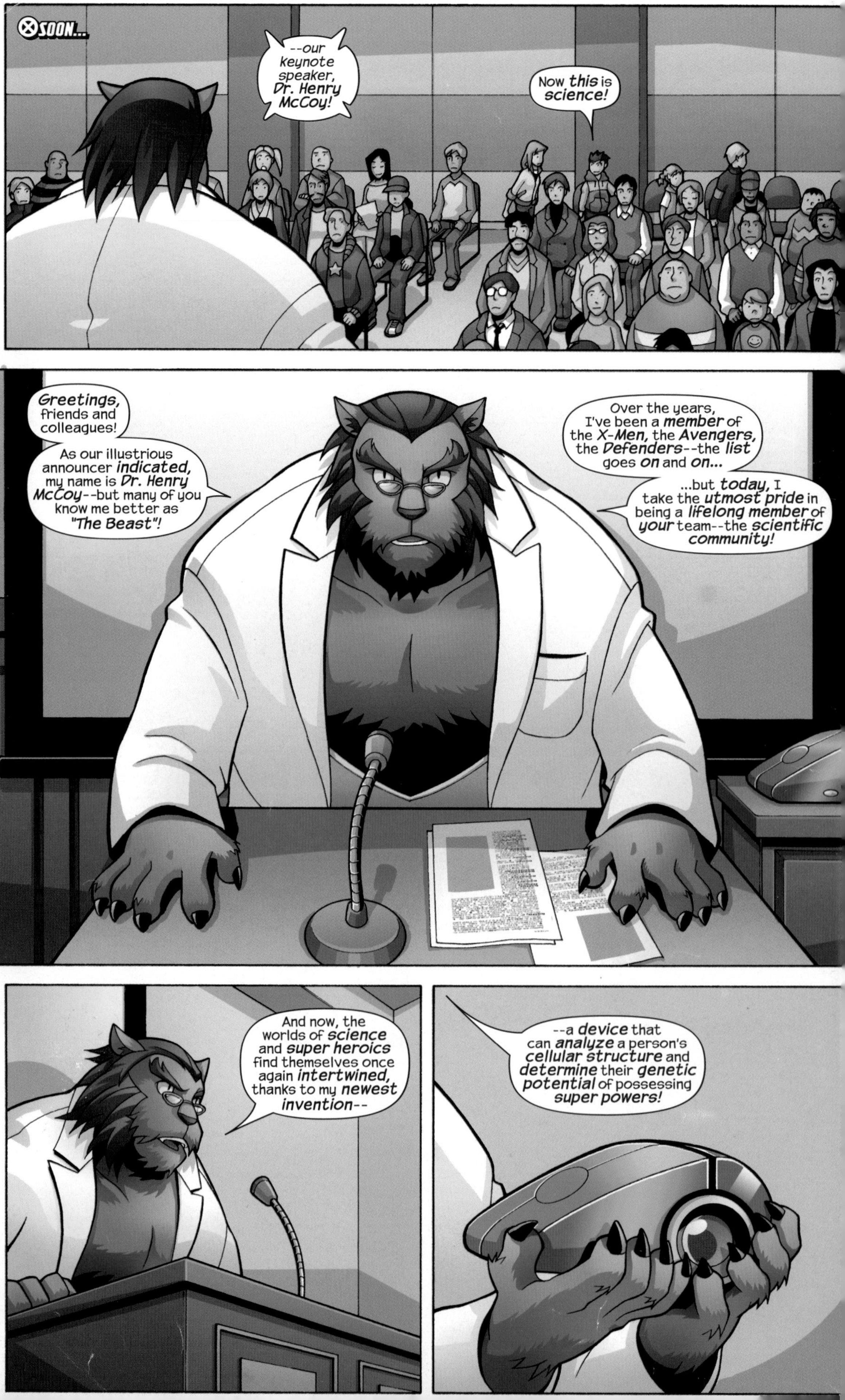
SOON...
--our keynote speaker, Dr. Henry McCoy!
Now this is science!
Greetings, friends and colleagues!
As our illustrious announcer indicated, my name is Dr. Henry McCoy--but many of you know me better as "The Beast"!
Over the years, I've been a member of the X-Men, the Avengers, the Defenders--the list goes on and on...
...but today, I take the utmost pride in being a lifelong member of your team--the scientific community!
And now, the worlds of science and super heroics find themselves once again intertwined, thanks to my newest invention--
--a device that can analyze a person's cellular structure and determine their genetic potential of possessing super powers!

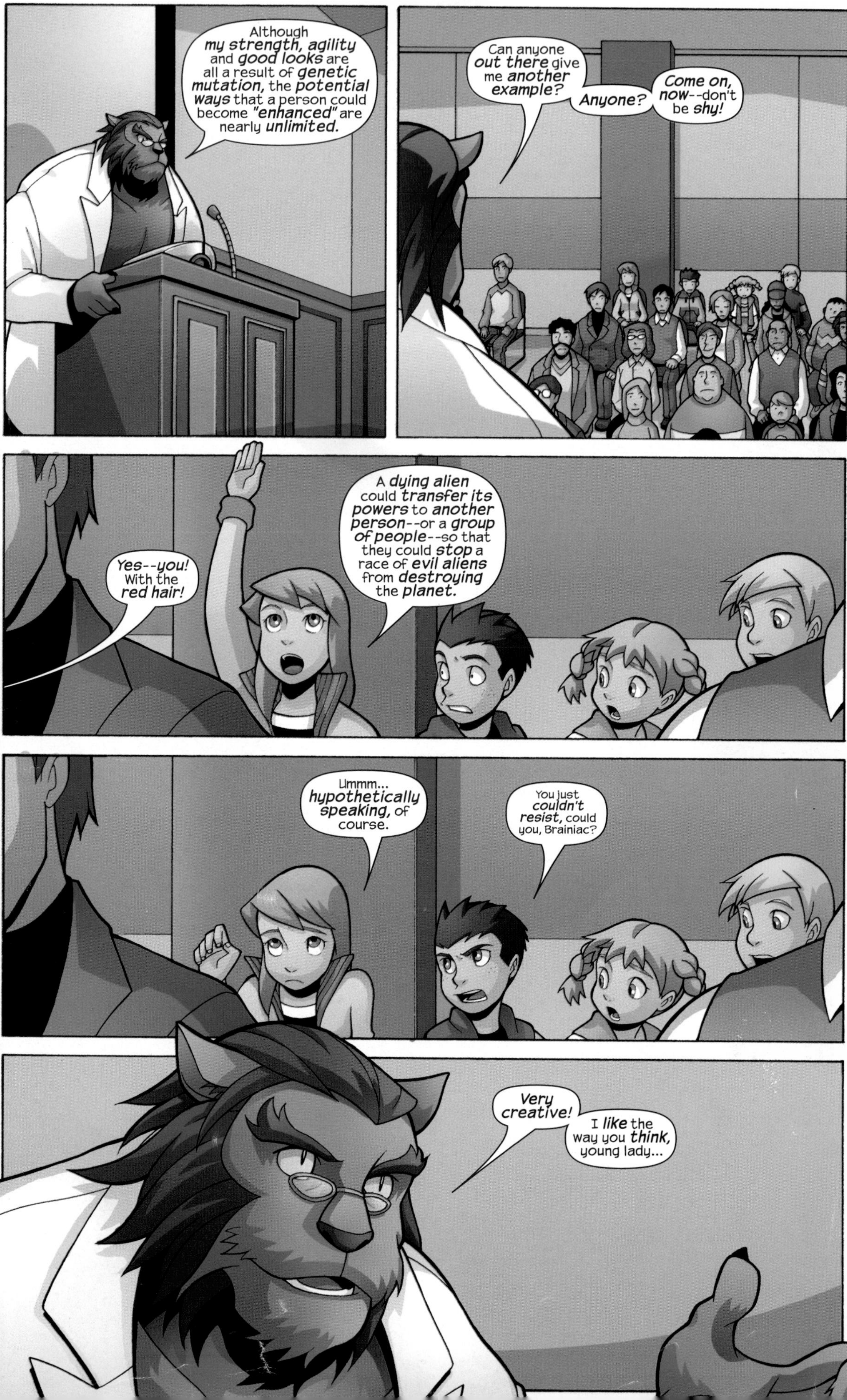

Although my strength, agility and good looks are all a result of genetic mutation, the potential ways that a person could become "enhanced" are nearly unlimited.
Can anyone out there give me another example?
Anyone?
Come on, now--don't be shy!
Yes--you! With the red hair!
A dying alien could transfer its powers to another person--or a group of people--so that they could stop a race of evil aliens from destroying the planet.
Ummm... hypothetically speaking, of course.
You just couldn't resist, could you, Brainiac?
Very creative!
I like the way you think, young lady...

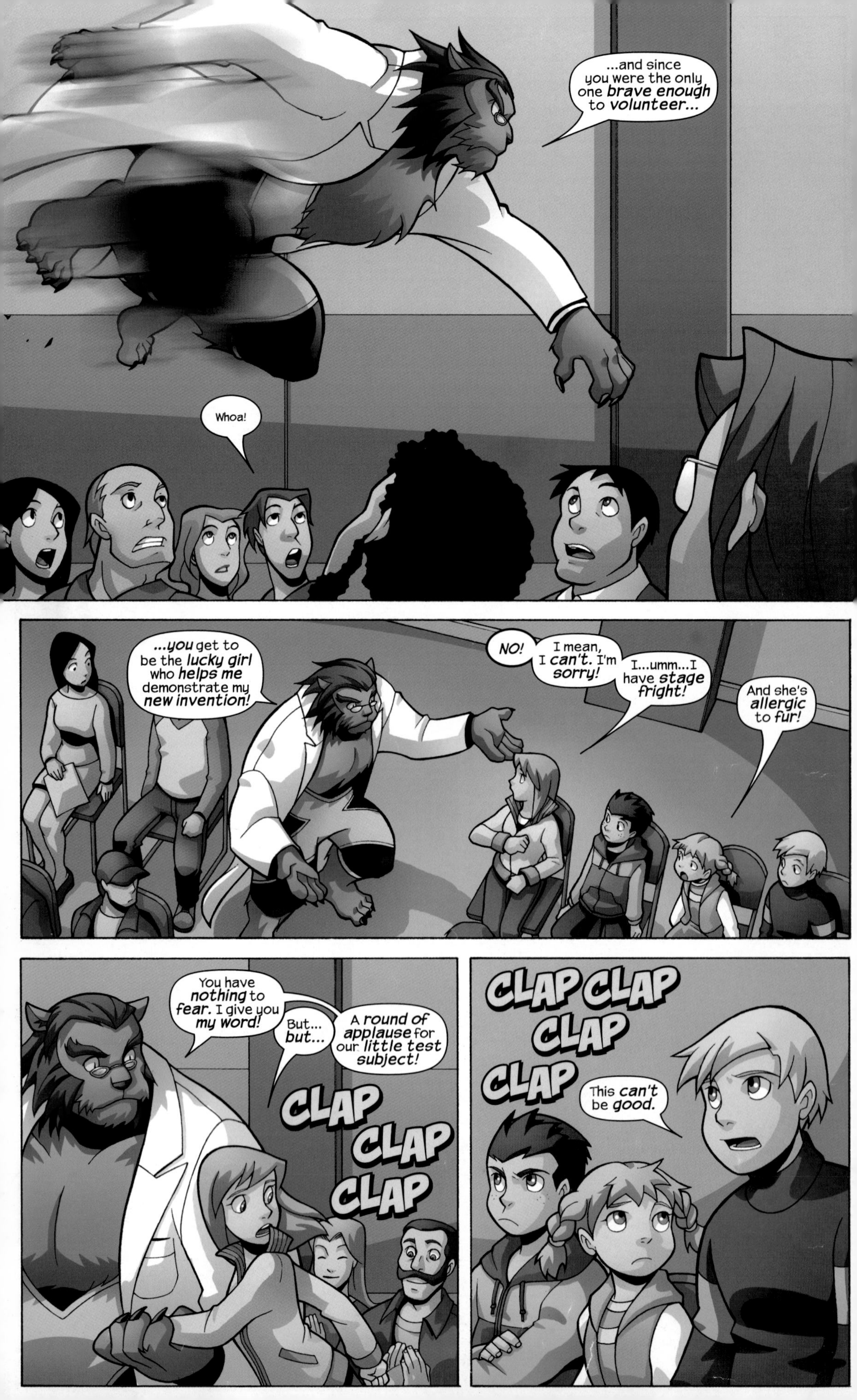

...and since you were the only one brave enough to volunteer...
Whoa!
...you get to be the lucky girl who helps me demonstrate my new invention!
NO!
I mean, I can't. I'm sorry!
I...umm...I have stage fright!
And she's allergic to fur!
You have nothing to fear. I give you my word!
But... but...
A round of applause for our little test subject!
CLAP CLAP CLAP
CLAP CLAP CLAP CLAP
This can't be good.

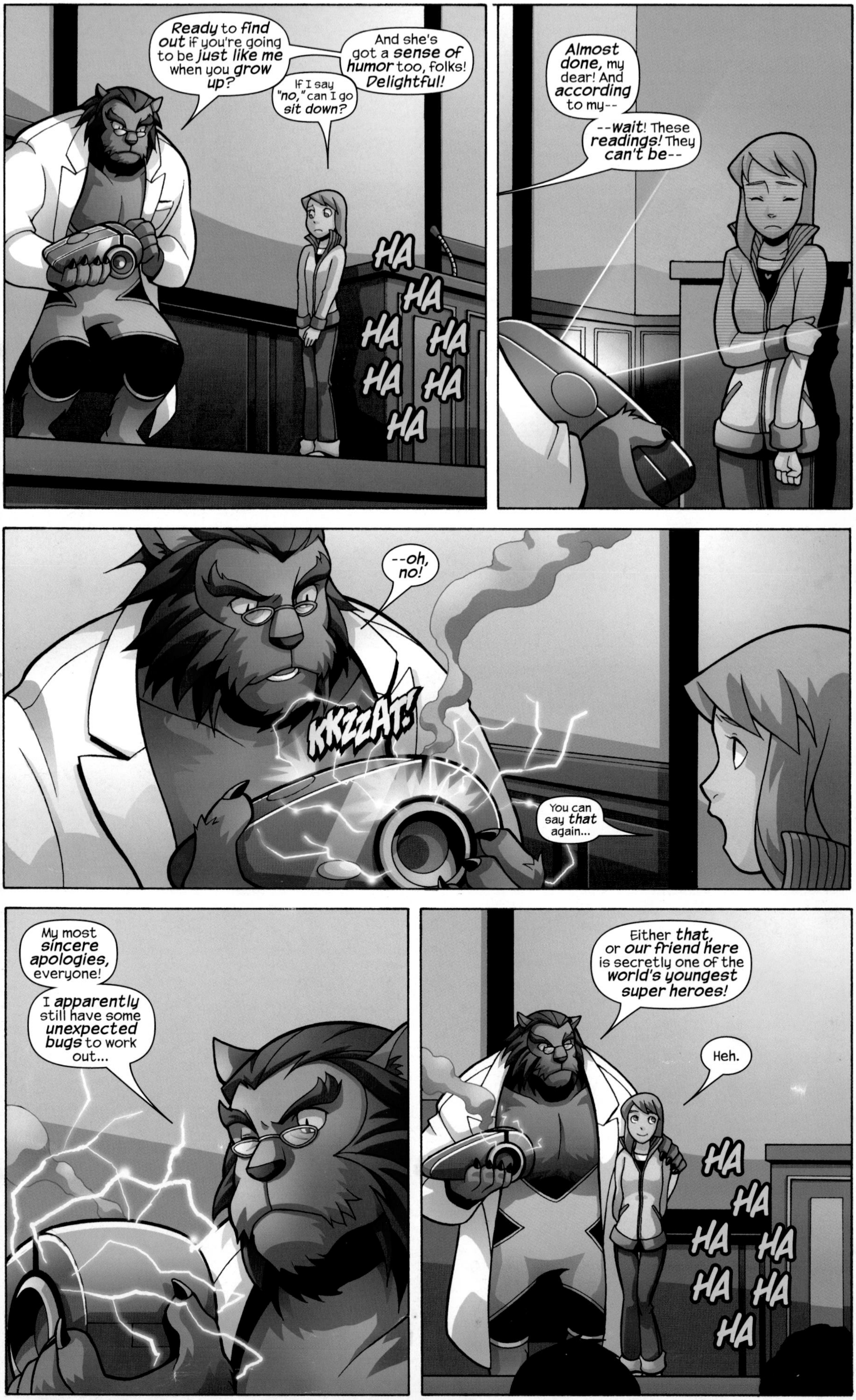
Ready to find out if you're going to be just like me when you grow up?
If I say "no," can I go sit down?
And she's got a sense of humor too, folks! Delightful!
HA HA HA HA HA HA HA
Almost done, my dear! And according to my--
--wait! These readings! They can't be--
--oh, no!
KKZZZAT!
You can say that again...
My most sincere apologies, everyone!
I apparently still have some unexpected bugs to work out...
Either that, or our friend here is secretly one of the world's youngest super heroes!
Heh.
HA HA HA HA HA HA HA

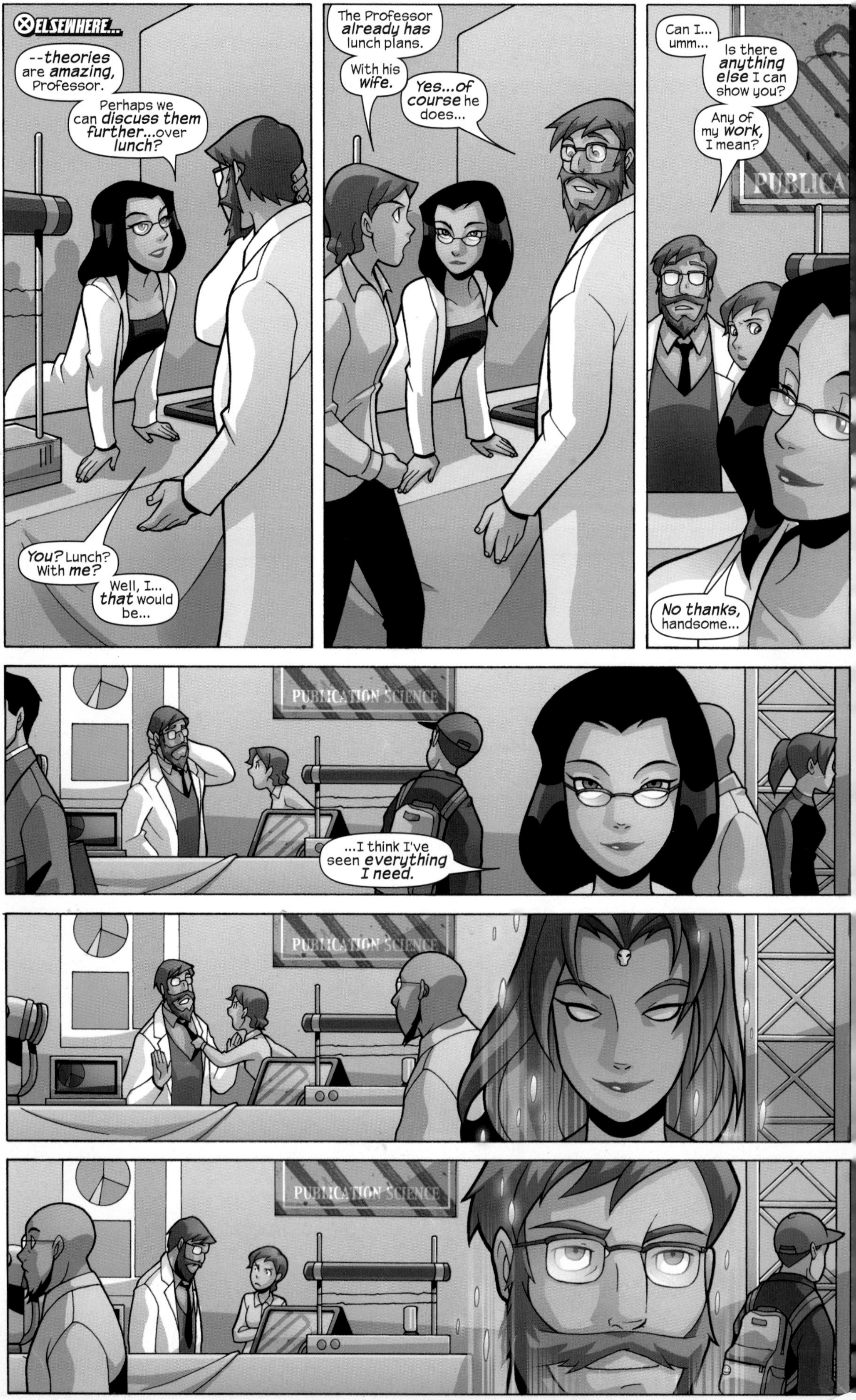
ELSEWHERE...
--theories are amazing, Professor.
Perhaps we can discuss them further...over lunch?
You? Lunch? With me?
Well, I... that would be...
The Professor already has lunch plans.
With his wife.
Yes...of course he does...
Can I... umm...
Is there anything else I can show you?
Any of my work, I mean?
PUBLICA
No thanks, handsome...
PUBLICATION SCIENCE
...I think I've seen everything I need.
PUBLICATION SCIENCE
PUBLICATION SCIENCE

--said I was *sorry*. I didn't *expect* him to pull me *on stage*.

Yeah, well, *we* didn't expect *you* to *reveal* our *secret origin*.

So, *hooray!* *Everyone* got a *surprise!*

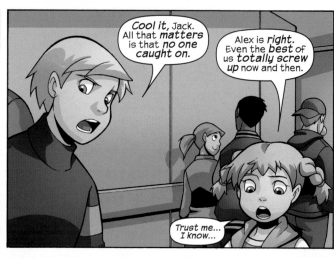

Cool it, Jack. All that *matters* is that *no one* caught on.

Alex is *right*. Even the *best* of us *totally screw up* now and then.

Trust me... I *know*...

Katie, I *didn't*--

Julie?

Hey, *Julie!*

Greg! What are *you*--

I saw you *up on stage!* That was *so cool!*

You got to meet a *real live X-Man!* I mean, how often does *that* happen?

More often than you'd *think*...

We're gonna go grab some *lunch*, Jules. You *coming?*

Why don't you guys *go ahead*. I'll *catch up* in a *few*.

If I *ever* get like *that* around a *boy*, I expect you to *put me out of my misery*.

Awww, do I *really* have to *wait that long?*

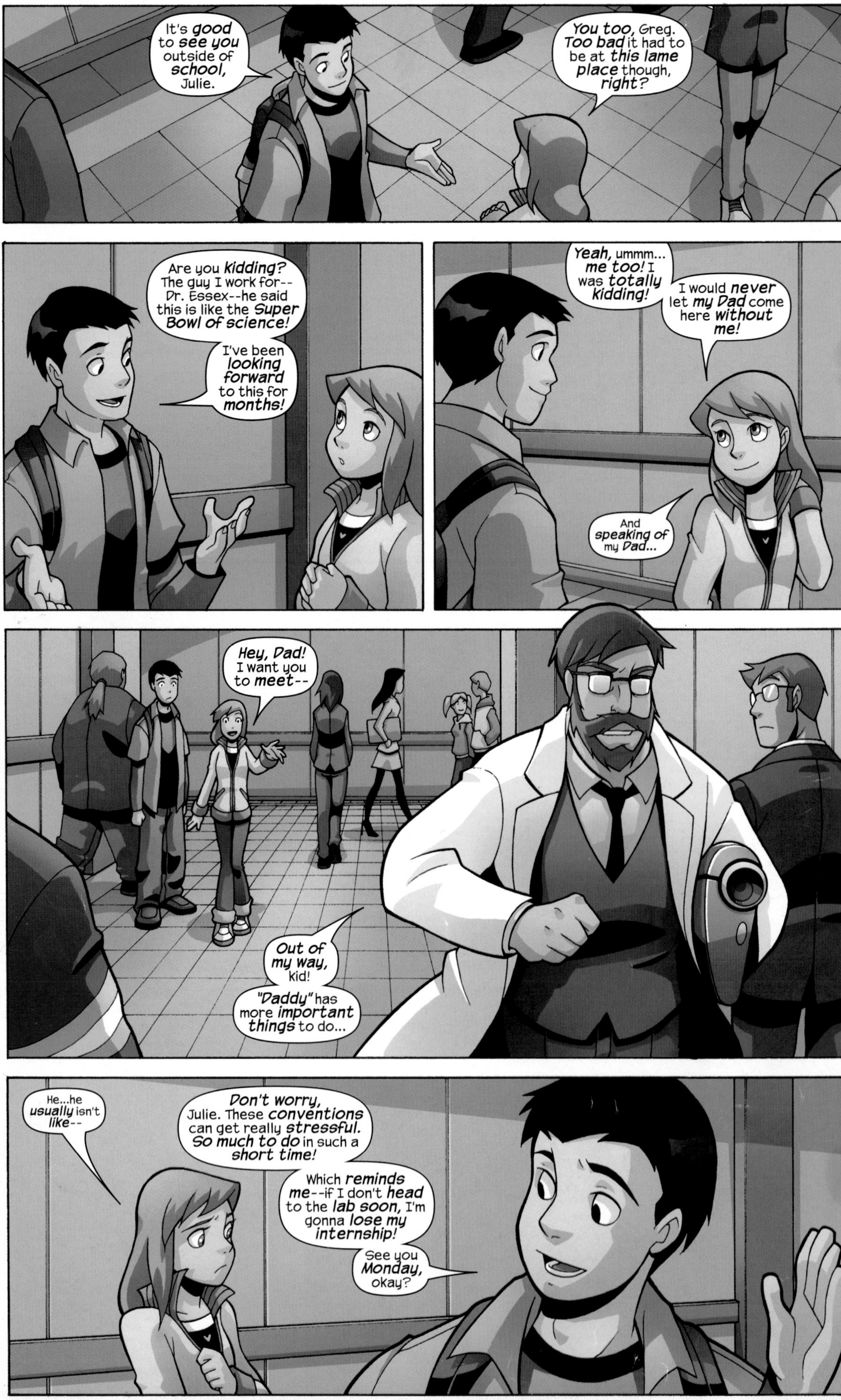
It's good to see you outside of school, Julie.
You too, Greg. Too bad it had to be at this lame place though, right?
Are you kidding? The guy I work for--Dr. Essex--he said this is like the Super Bowl of science!
I've been looking forward to this for months!
Yeah, ummm... me too! I was totally kidding!
I would never let my Dad come here without me!
And speaking of my Dad...
Hey, Dad! I want you to meet--
Out of my way, kid!
"Daddy" has more important things to do...
He...he usually isn't like--
Don't worry, Julie. These conventions can get really stressful. So much to do in such a short time!
Which reminds me--if I don't head to the lab soon, I'm gonna lose my internship!
See you Monday, okay?

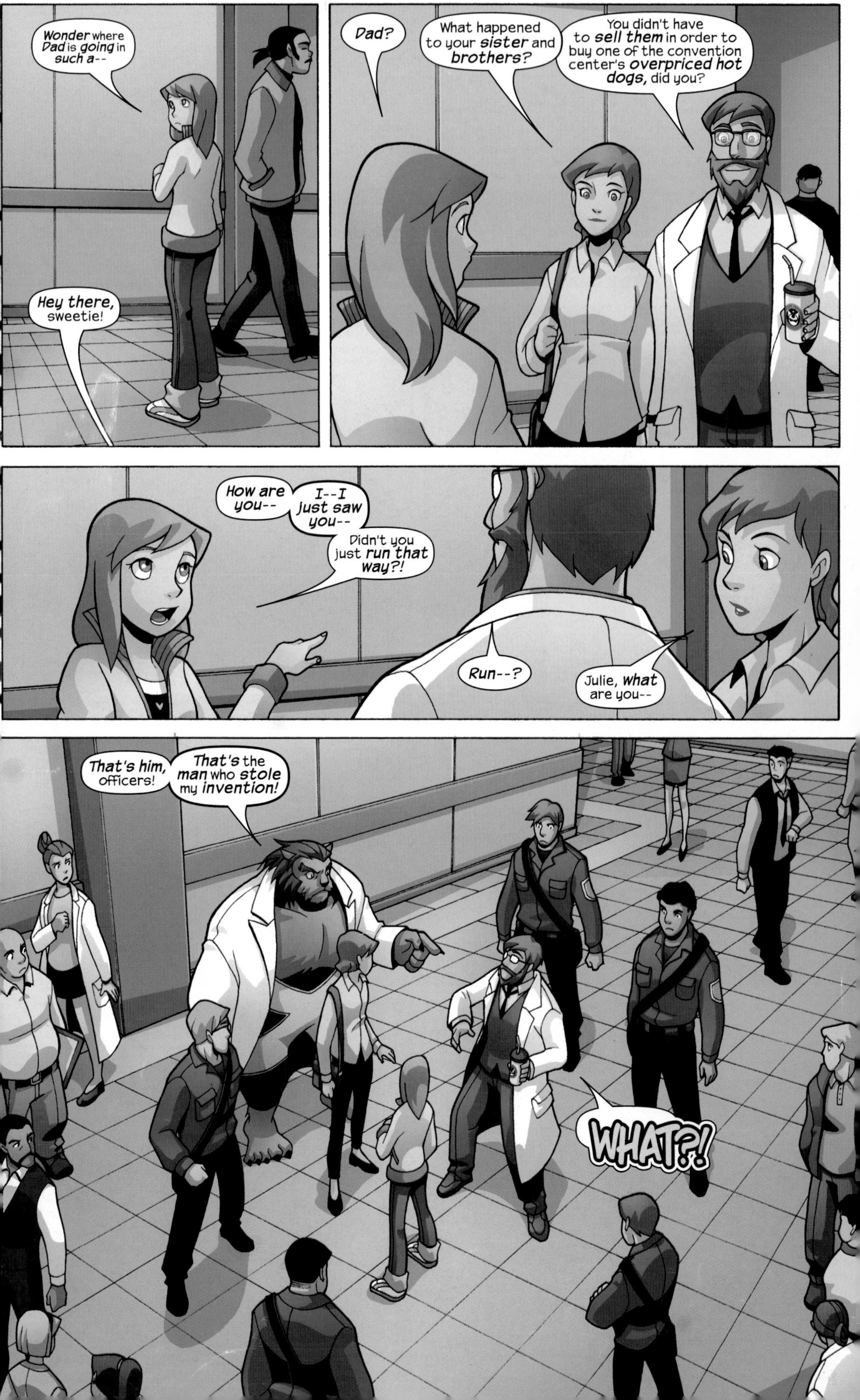

Wonder where Dad is going in such a--
Hey there, sweetie!
Dad?
What happened to your sister and brothers?
You didn't have to sell them in order to buy one of the convention center's overpriced hot dogs, did you?
How are you--
I--I just saw you--
Didn't you just run that way?!
Run--?
Julie, what are you--
That's him, officers!
That's the man who stole my invention!
WHAT?!

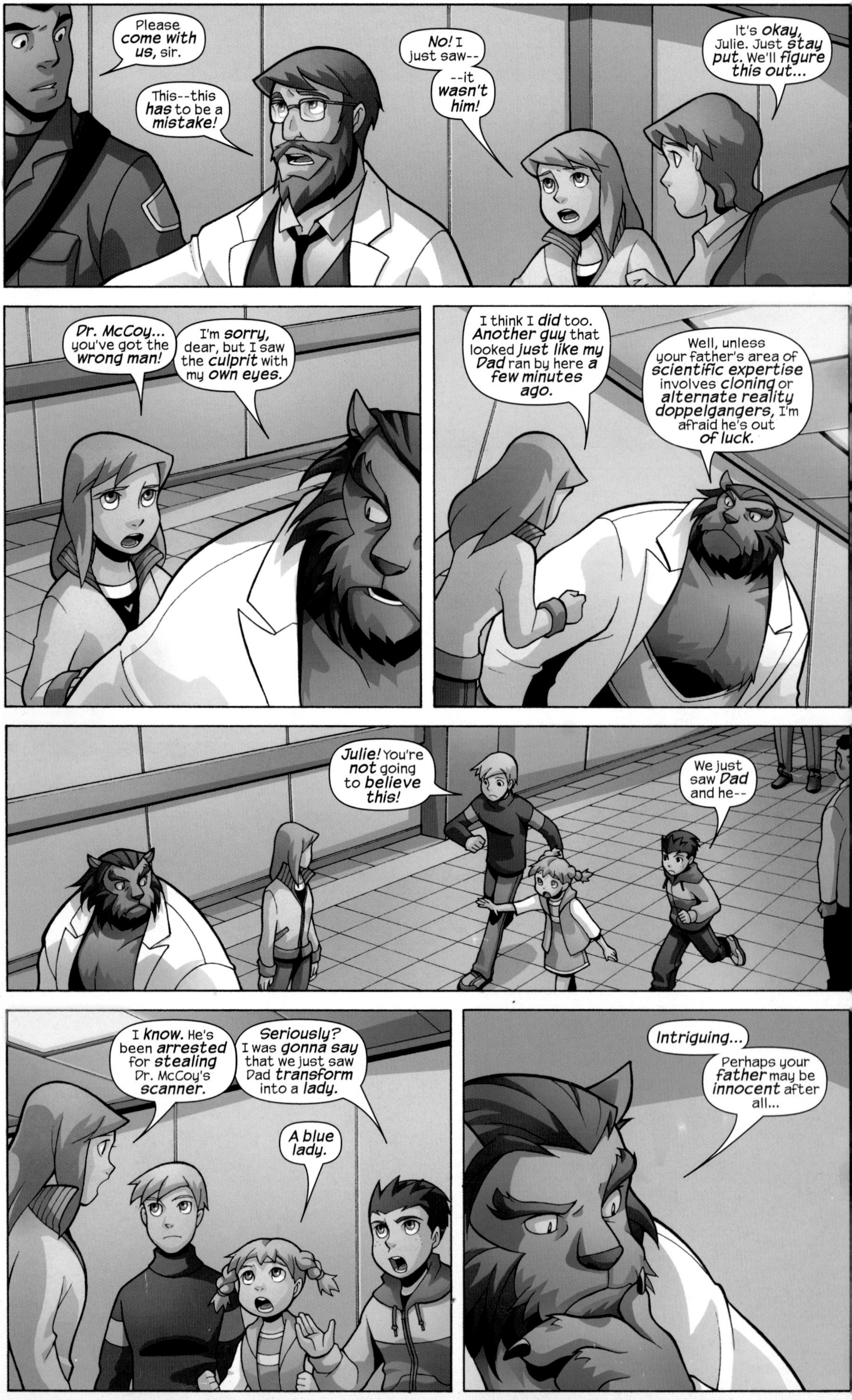

Please come with us, sir.
This--this has to be a mistake!
No! I just saw--
--it wasn't him!
It's okay, Julie. Just stay put. We'll figure this out...
Dr. McCoy... you've got the wrong man!
I'm sorry, dear, but I saw the culprit with my own eyes.
I think I did too. Another guy that looked just like my Dad ran by here a few minutes ago.
Well, unless your father's area of scientific expertise involves cloning or alternate reality doppelgangers, I'm afraid he's out of luck.
Julie! You're not going to believe this!
We just saw Dad and he--
I know. He's been arrested for stealing Dr. McCoy's scanner.
Seriously? I was gonna say that we just saw Dad transform into a lady.
A blue lady.
Intriguing...
Perhaps your father may be innocent after all...

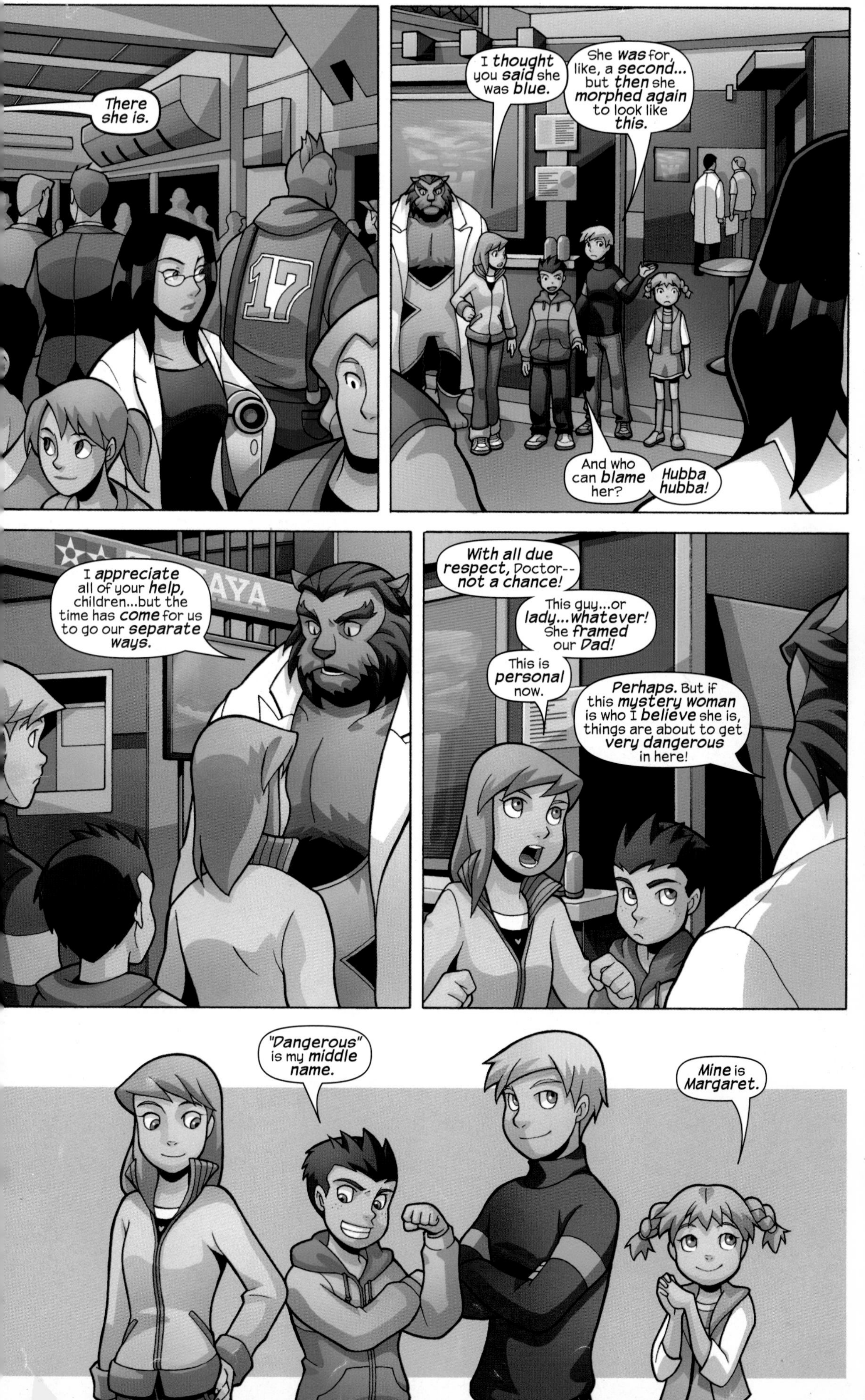
There she is.
I thought you said she was blue.
She was for, like, a second... but then she morphed again to look like this.
And who can blame her?
Hubba hubba!
I appreciate all of your help, children...but the time has come for us to go our separate ways.
With all due respect, Doctor-- not a chance!
This guy...or lady...whatever! She framed our Dad!
This is personal now.
Perhaps. But if this mystery woman is who I believe she is, things are about to get very dangerous in here!
"Dangerous" is my middle name.
Mine is Margaret.

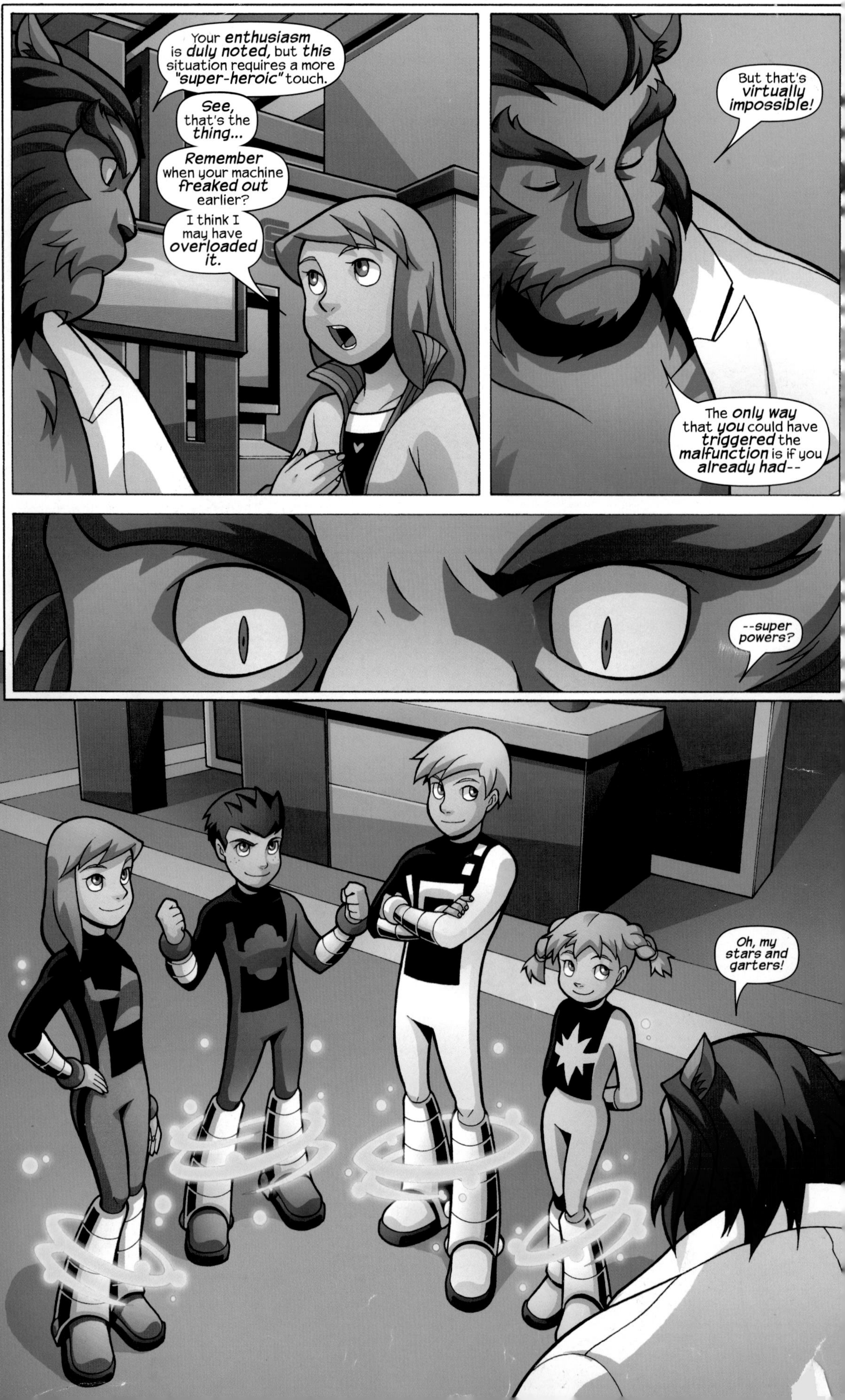
Your enthusiasm is duly noted, but this situation requires a more "super-heroic" touch.
See, that's the thing...
Remember when your machine freaked out earlier?
I think I may have overloaded it.
But that's virtually impossible!
The only way that you could have triggered the malfunction is if you already had--
--super powers?
Oh, my stars and garters!

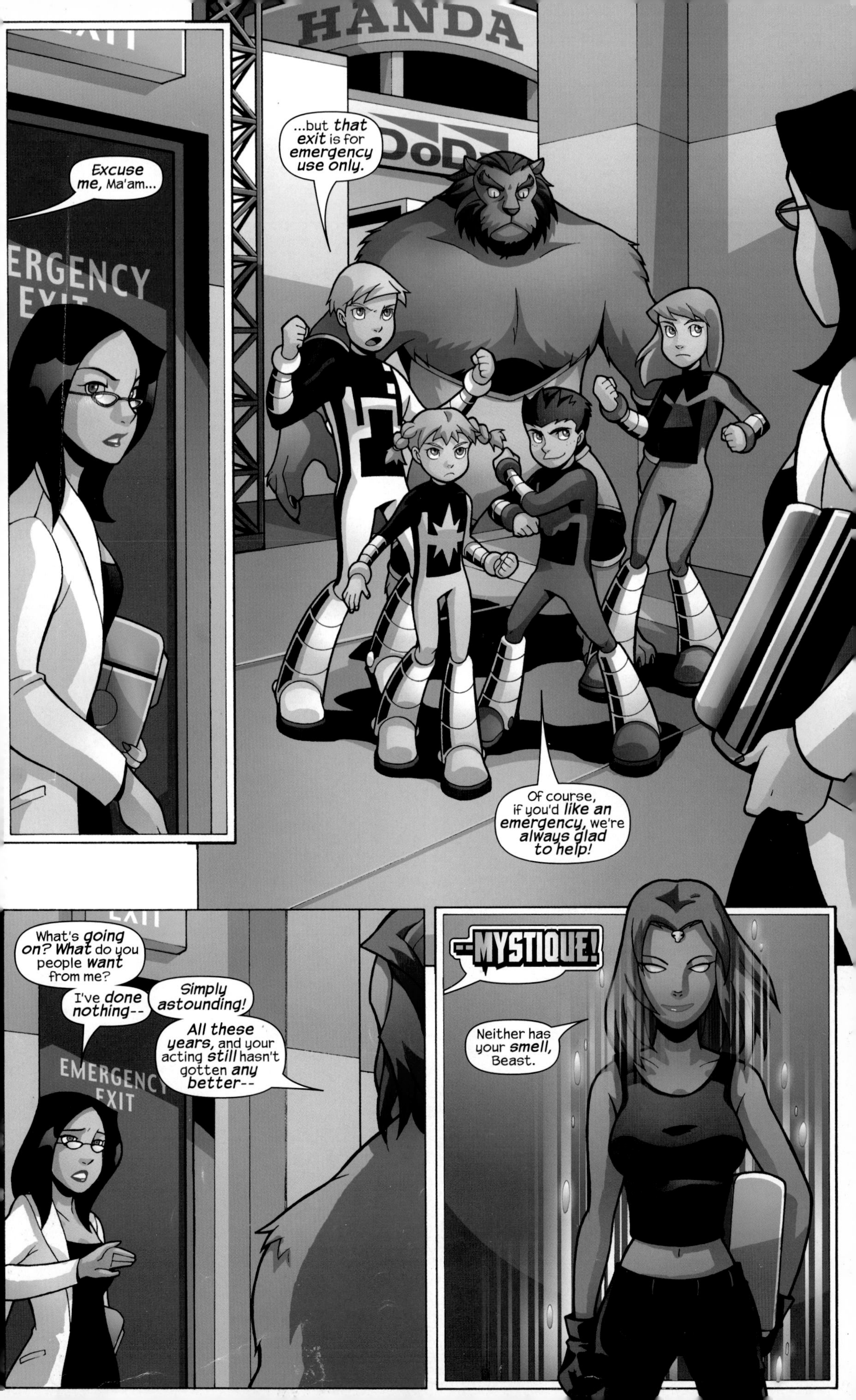

HANDA
Excuse me, Ma'am...
...but that exit is for emergency use only.
EMERGENCY EXIT
Of course, if you'd like an emergency, we're always glad to help!
EXIT
What's going on? What do you people want from me?
I've done nothing--
Simply astounding!
All these years, and your acting still hasn't gotten any better--
EMERGENCY EXIT
--MYSTIQUE!
Neither has your smell, Beast.

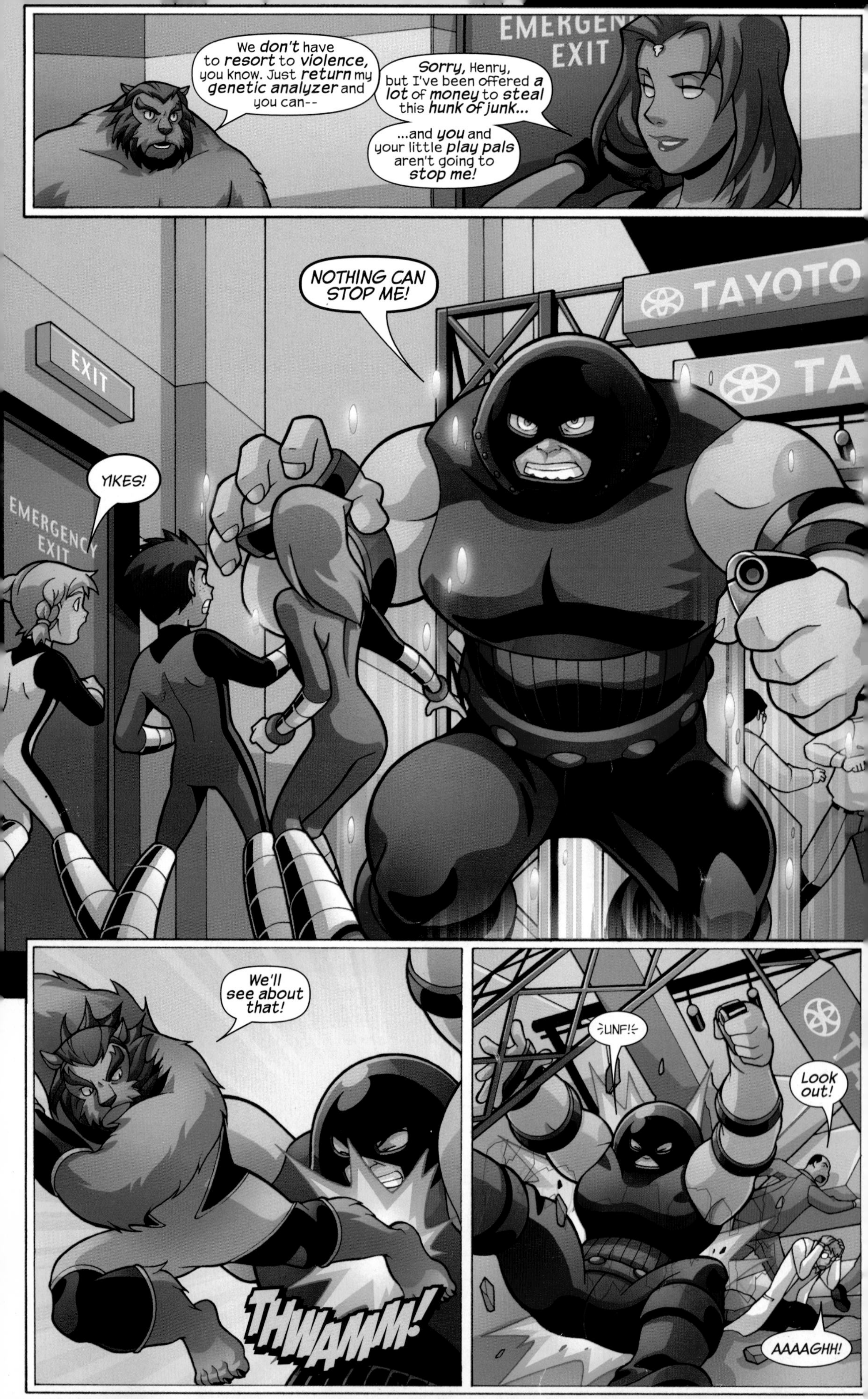
We don't have to resort to violence, you know. Just return my genetic analyzer and you can--
Sorry, Henry, but I've been offered a lot of money to steal this hunk of junk...
...and you and your little play pals aren't going to stop me!
EMERGENCY EXIT
NOTHING CAN STOP ME!
TAYOTO
EXIT
EMERGENCY EXIT
YIKES!
We'll see about that!
THWAMM!
UNF!
Look out!
AAAAGHH!

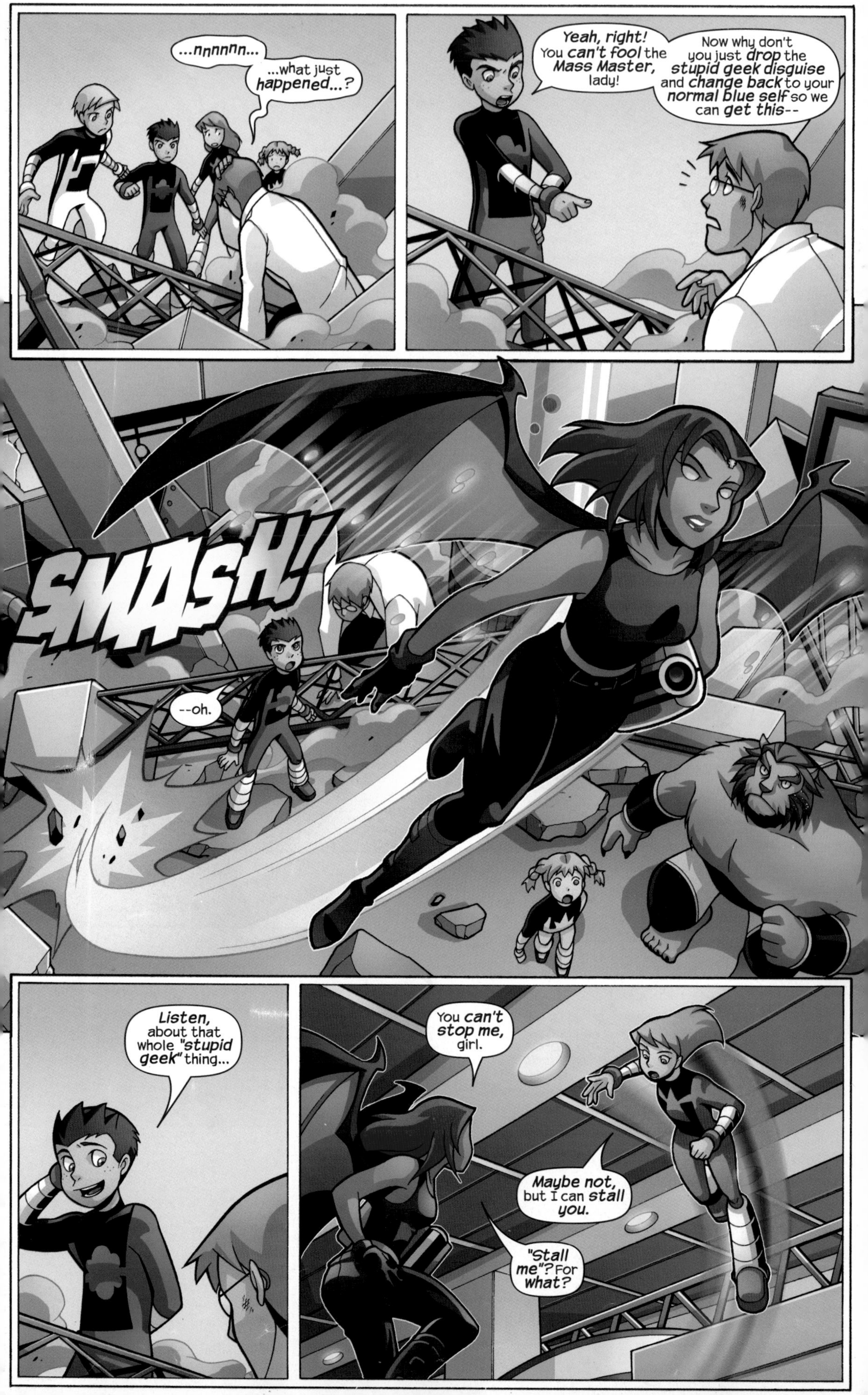
...nnnnnn...
...what just happened...?
Yeah, right! You can't fool the Mass Master, lady!
Now why don't you just drop the stupid geek disguise and change back to your normal blue self so we can get this--
SMASH!!
--oh.
Listen, about that whole "stupid geek" thing...
You can't stop me, girl.
Maybe not, but I can stall you.
"Stall me"? For what?

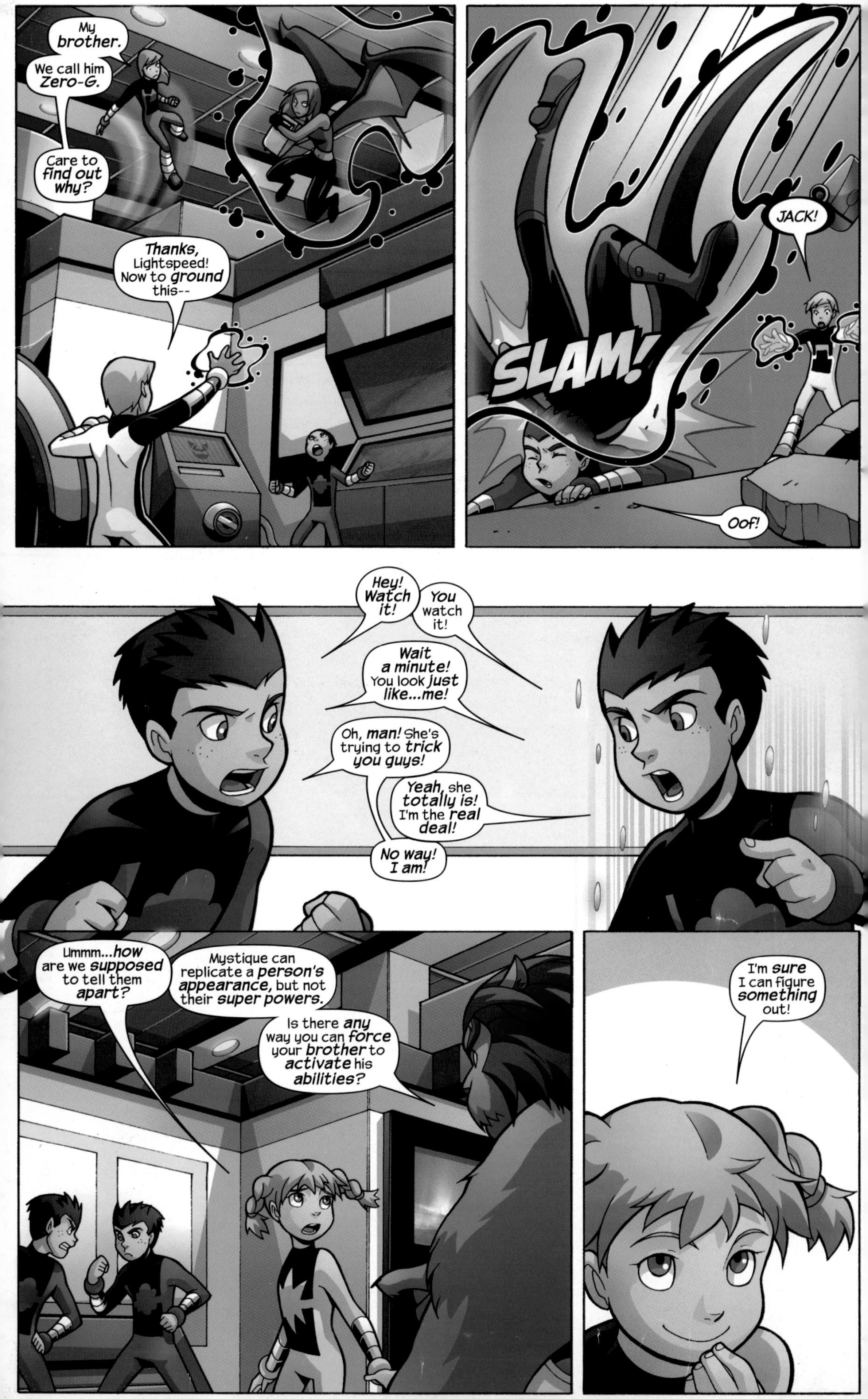

My brother.
We call him Zero-G.
Care to find out why?
Thanks, Lightspeed! Now to ground this--
SLAM!
JACK!
Oof!
Hey! Watch it!
You watch it!
Wait a minute! You look just like...me!
Oh, man! She's trying to trick you guys!
Yeah, she totally is! I'm the real deal!
No way! I am!
Ummm...how are we supposed to tell them apart?
Mystique can replicate a person's appearance, but not their super powers.
Is there any way you can force your brother to activate his abilities?
I'm sure I can figure something out!

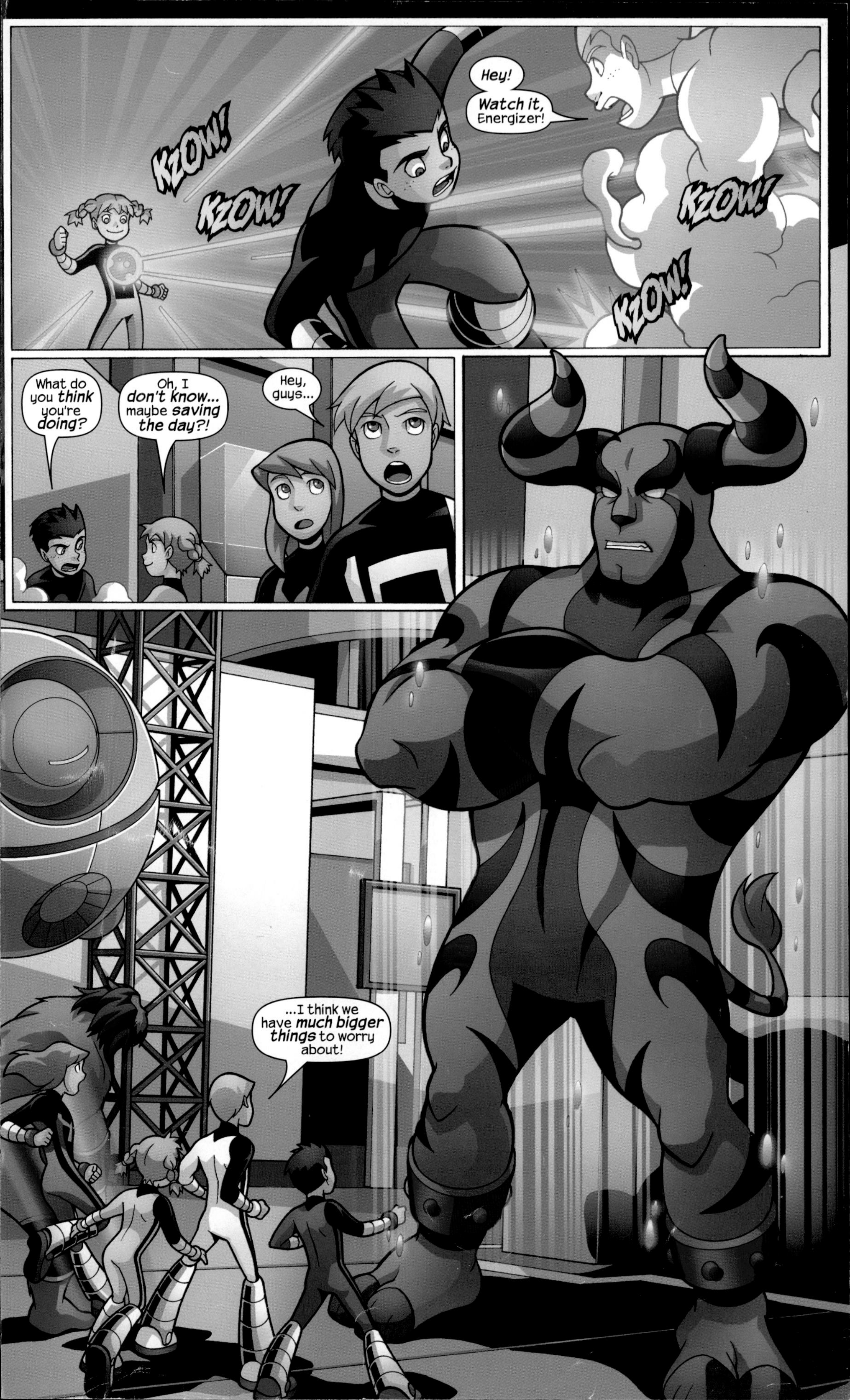
KZOW!
KZOW!
Hey!
Watch it, Energizer!
KZOW!
KZOW!
What do you think you're doing?
Oh, I don't know... maybe saving the day?!
Hey, guys...
...I think we have much bigger things to worry about!

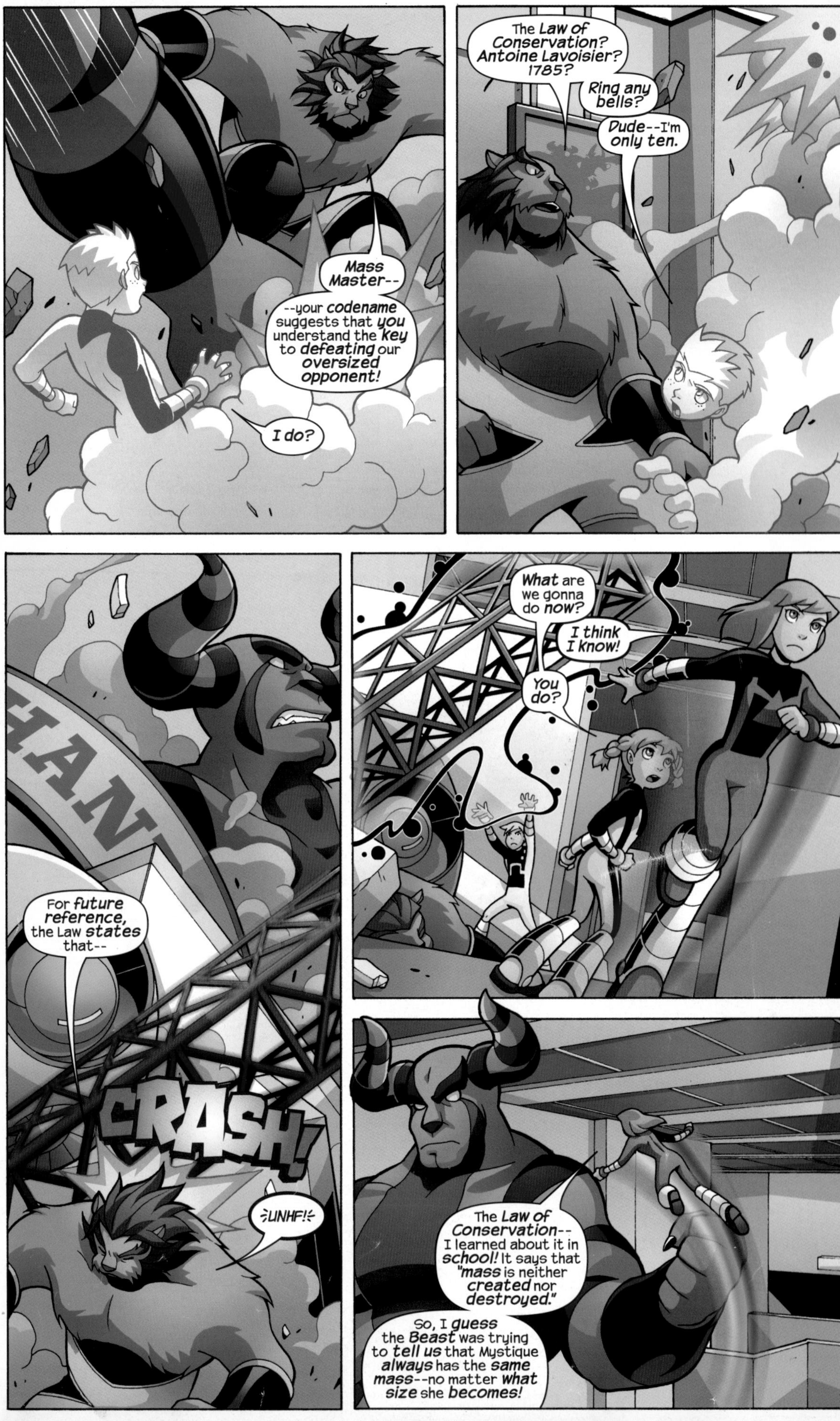
Mass Master--
--your codename suggests that you understand the key to defeating our oversized opponent!
I do?
The Law of Conservation? Antoine Lavoisier? 1785?
Ring any bells?
Dude--I'm only ten.
For future reference, the Law states that--
CRASH!
UNHF!
What are we gonna do now?
I think I know!
You do?
The Law of Conservation-- I learned about it in school! It says that "mass is neither created nor destroyed."
So, I guess the Beast was trying to tell us that Mystique always has the same mass--no matter what size she becomes!

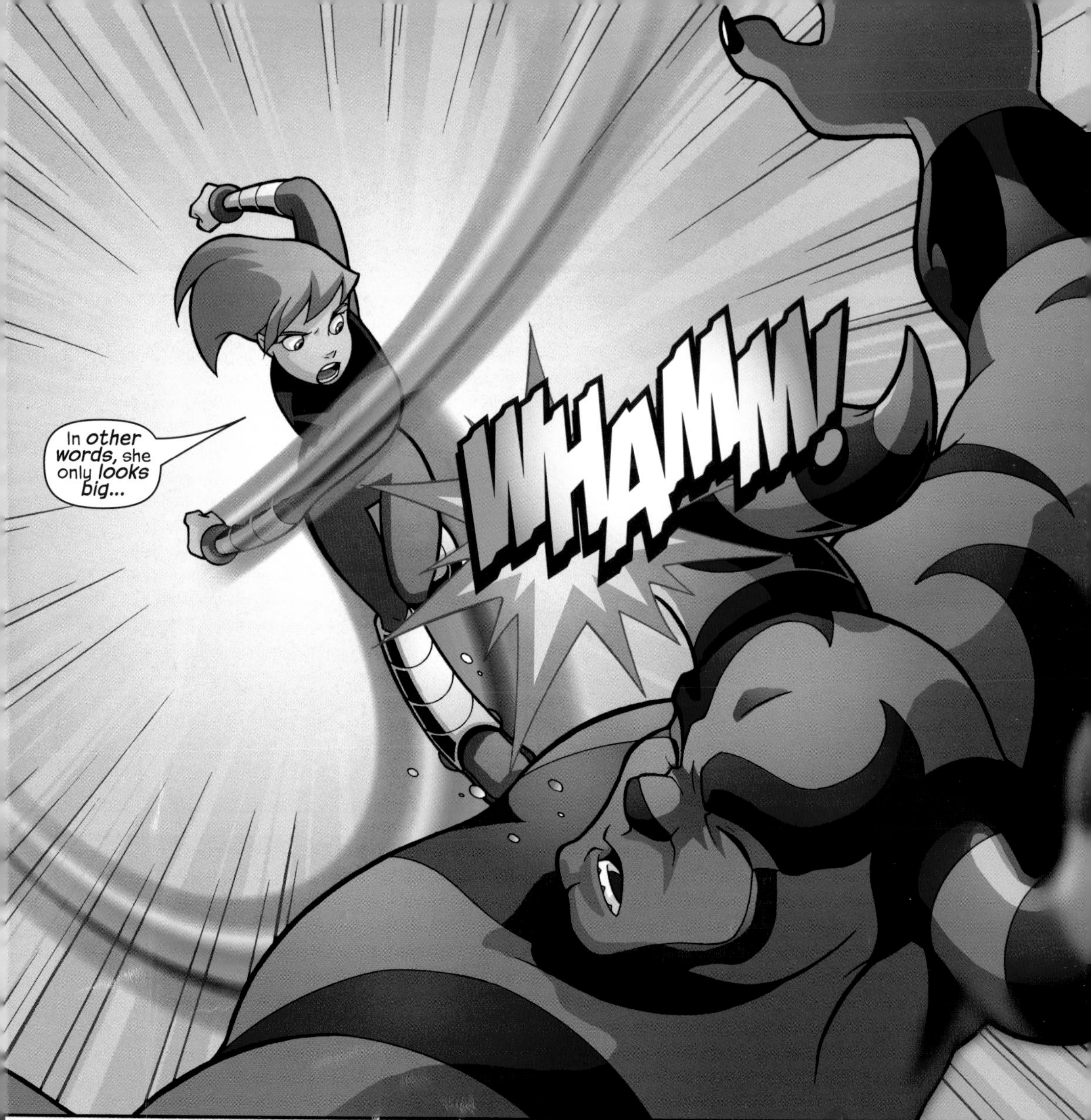
In other words, she only looks big...
WHAMM!

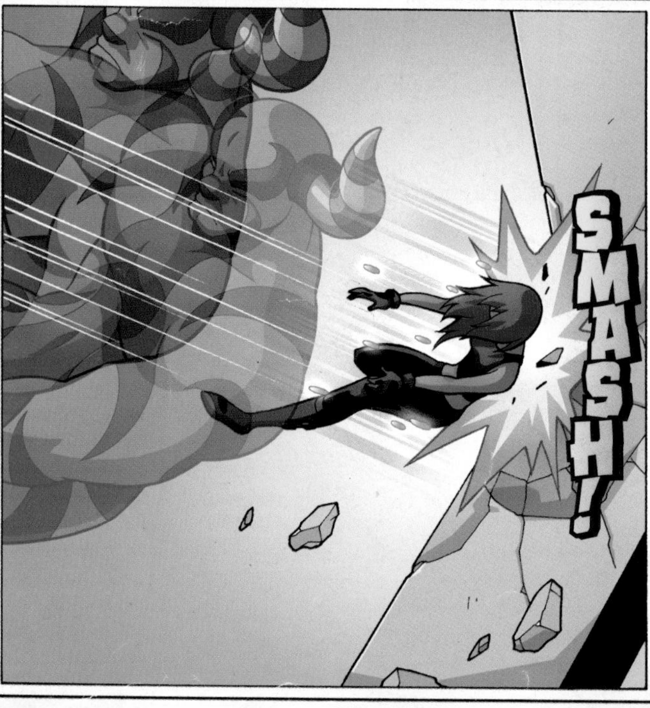
SMASH!

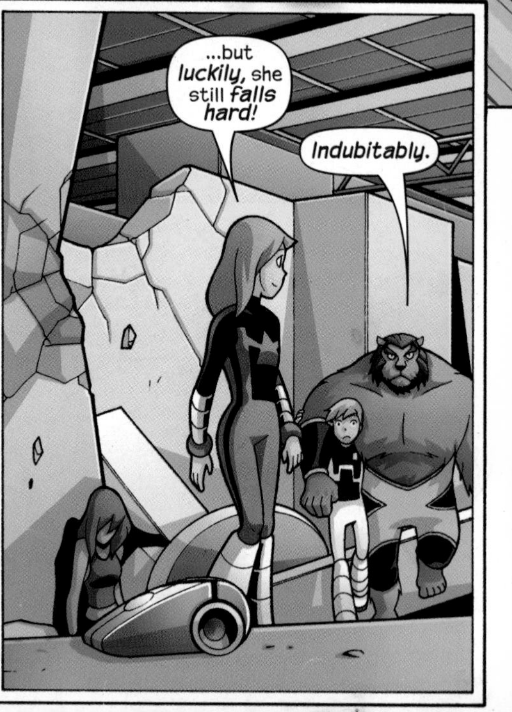
...but luckily, she still falls hard!
Indubitably.

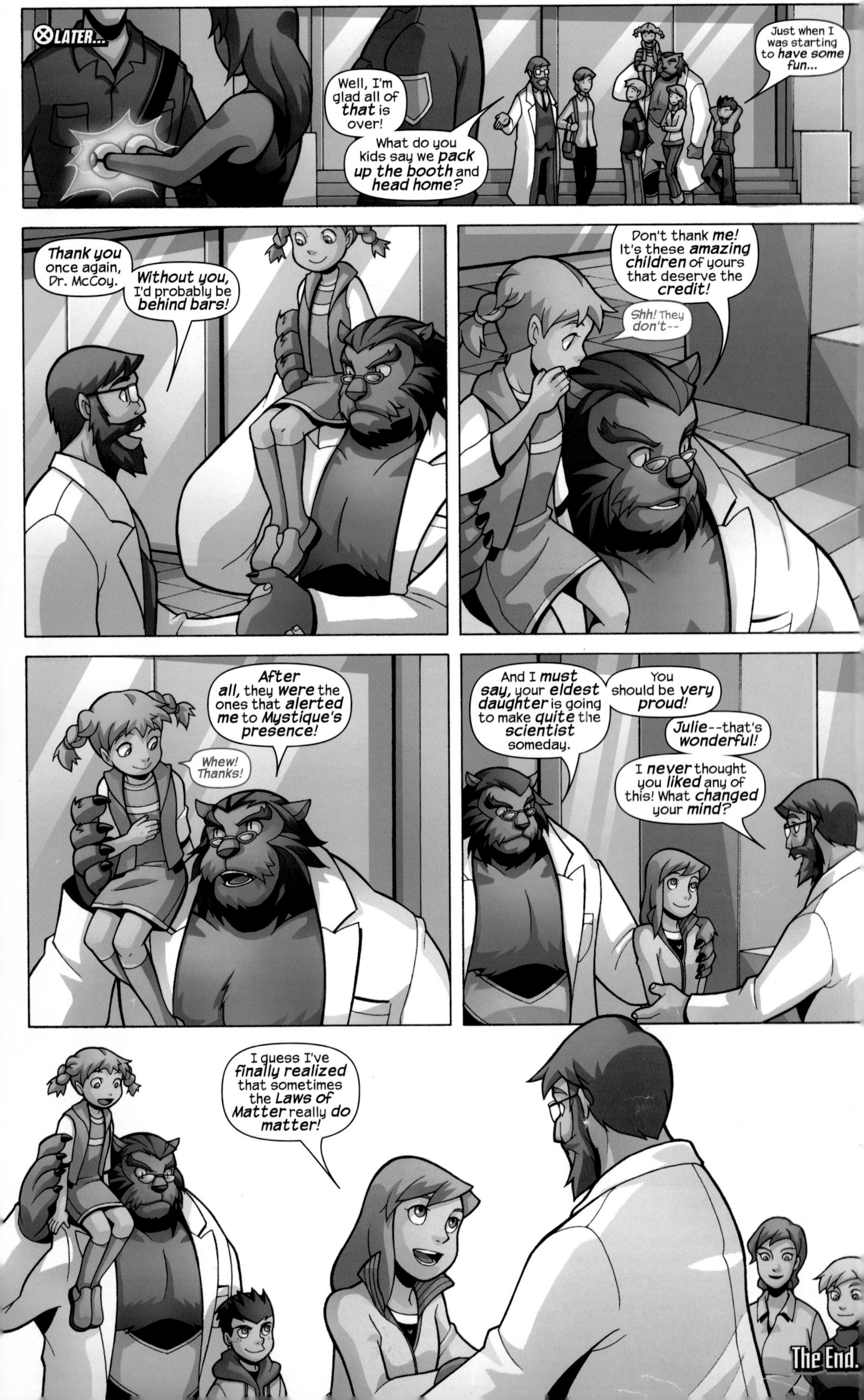
LATER...
Well, I'm glad all of that is over!
What do you kids say we pack up the booth and head home?
Just when I was starting to have some fun...
Thank you once again, Dr. McCoy.
Without you, I'd probably be behind bars!
Don't thank me! It's these amazing children of yours that deserve the credit!
Shh! They don't--
After all, they were the ones that alerted me to Mystique's presence!
Whew! Thanks!
And I must say, your eldest daughter is going to make quite the scientist someday.
You should be very proud!
Julie--that's wonderful!
I never thought you liked any of this! What changed your mind?
I guess I've finally realized that sometimes the Laws of Matter really do matter!
The End.